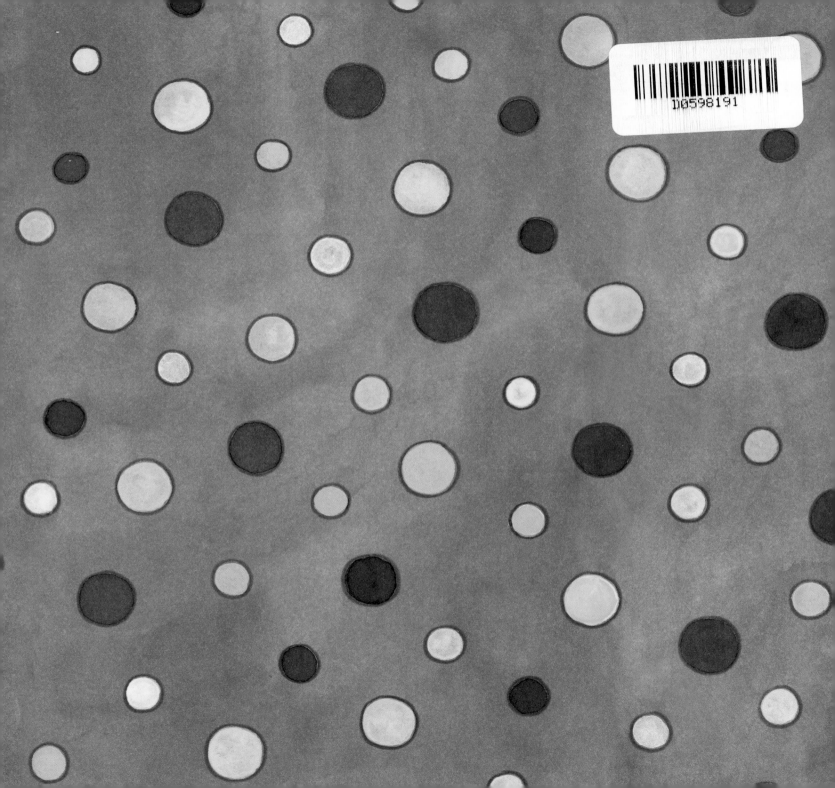

BIG
CAT,
little cat

Elisha Cooper

ROARING BROOK PRESS
NEW YORK

There was a cat

who lived alone.

Until the day

a new cat came.

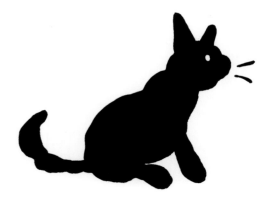

The cat showed the new
cat what to do.

When to eat,

when to drink,

where to go,

how to be,

when to rest.

Big cat, little cat.

Days went by—and months, too—and the little cat grew

and grew

and grew.

Big cat, bigger cat.

The cats lived in the
city and every day
there was work.

Cooking,

cleaning,

climbing,

hunting,

exploring,

making plans.

For five minutes each day

they went wild.

Afterward they dreamed.

Their days were full.

Years went by—
and more years, too—

and every day the cats
were together.

Until the older cat got older

and one day he had to go . . .

and he didn't come back.

And that was hard.

For everyone.

Until the day a new cat came.

The cat showed the
new cat what to do.

When to eat,

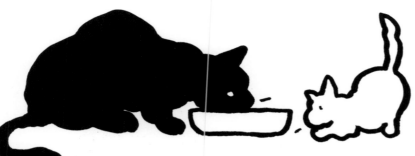

when to drink,

where to go,

how to be,

when to rest.

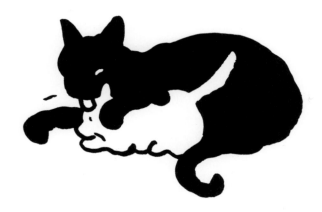

Big cat, little cat.

For Moppet, Harry, Keeper, Miss Muffet, Daisy, McGillivray, Stubbs,

Brutus, Ferdinand, Fiasco, Acorn, Ovid, Ivy, Dido, Aeneas, Garfield,

Skunky, Hickory, Homer, Emma, Neeka, Badger, Gaddis, Sophie,

Henry, Caleb, Hannah, Turtle, Bear, and Mouse

Copyright © 2017 by Elisha Cooper
Published by Roaring Brook Press
Roaring Brook Press is a division of Holtzbrinck Publishing Holdings Limited Partnership
175 Fifth Avenue, New York, NY 10010

mackids.com

Library of Congress Cataloging-in-Publication Data

Names: Cooper, Elisha, author.
Title: Big cat, little cat / Elisha Cooper.
Description: First edition. | New York : Roaring Brook Press, 2017. | Summary: "A moving tale about friendship, new beginnings, and cats"—Provided by publisher.
Identifiers: LCCN 2016002014 | ISBN 9781626723719 (hardback)
Subjects: | CYAC: Cats—Fiction. | Friendship—Fiction. | BISAC: JUVENILE FICTION / Animals / Cats. | JUVENILE FICTION / Social Issues / Death & Dying. | JUVENILE FICTION / Family / Multigenerational.
Classification: LCC PZ7.C784737 Bi 2017 | DDC [E]—dc23
LC record available at https://lccn.loc.gov/2016002014

Our books may be purchased in bulk for promotional, educational, or business use. Please contact your local bookseller or the Macmillan Corporate and Premium Sales Department at (800) 221-7945 ext. 5442 or by e-mail at MacmillanSpecialMarkets@macmillan.com.

First edition, 2017
Printed in China by Toppan Leefung Printing Ltd., Dongguan City, Guangdong Province

5 7 9 10 8 6 4

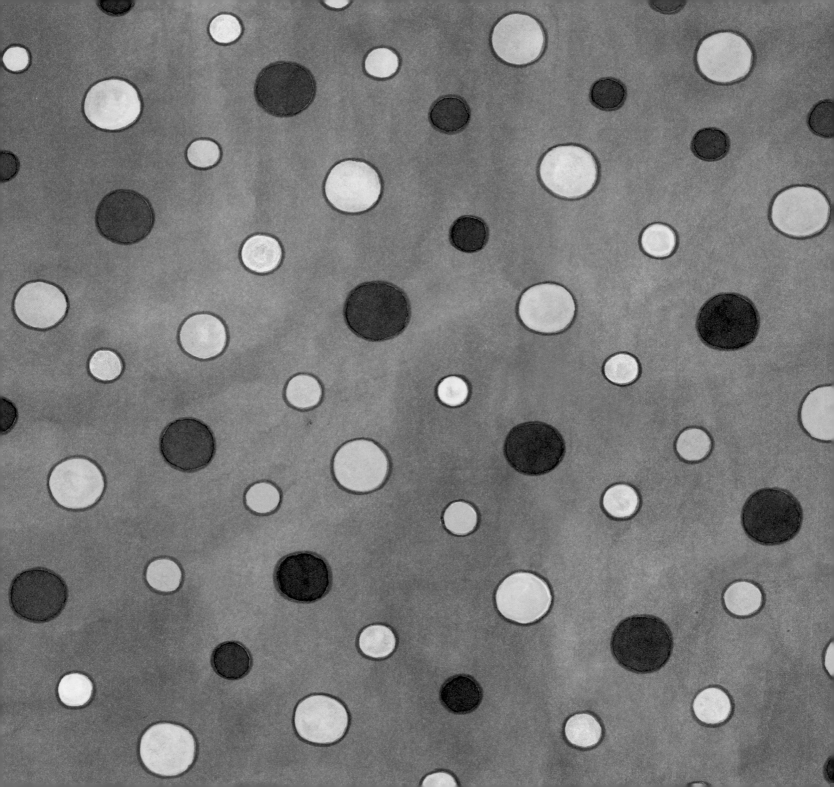